Being a Good Friend

Nunavummi

The Nunavummi reading series is a Nunavut-developed levelled book series that supports literacy development while teaching readers about the people, traditions, and environment of the Canadian Arctic.

Published in Canada by Nunavummi, an imprint of Inhabit Education Books Inc. | www.inhabiteducation.com

Inhabit Education Books Inc.
(Iqaluit), P.O. Box 2129, Iqaluit, Nunavut, X0A 1H0
(Toronto), 191 Eglinton Avenue East, Suite 301, Toronto, Ontario, M4P 1K1

Design and layout copyright © 2019 Inhabit Education Books Inc.
Text copyright © Neil Christopher
Illustrations by Amanda Sandland © Inhabit Education Books Inc.

Printed in Canada.

ISBN: 978-0-2287-0277-1

INHABIT
EDUCATION

Being a
Good Friend

WRITTEN BY
Neil Christopher

ILLUSTRATED BY
Amanda Sandland

Uka woke up and jumped out of bed. He looked out his window and saw that the sky was clear and the sun was already high in the sky.

A perfect day for biking! Today was the day he and Sissi had planned to go on a bike trip.

Uka hurried to get ready for the trip. "I can't wait to go biking!" Uka said to himself.

Uka dressed quickly.

He had a healthy breakfast of eggs and toast. Then he washed his face and brushed his teeth. Uka gathered some delicious snacks and a thermos of tea for their trip. He put them in his backpack. Now that he had what he needed, Uka put on his bike helmet and went outside.

Uka straightened the mirrors on the bike and checked the tires.

Everything looked good, and Uka started on his way. He was ready to bike to Sissi's house!

Uka was excited to be outside in the fresh air. He waved at Tuka and Umi. They were going to the river to fish.

He biked past Aqi and Ukpik. They were out for a walk.

"Aqi and Ukpik!" Uka yelled. The friends smiled and waved back at him. Uka was biking quickly, so it didn't take him long to get to Sissi's house.

When he arrived, Uka jumped off of his bike and ran to the door.

"Sissi! Sissi!" he called.

"Sissi! I am here!" he yelled again.

Sissi's mother opened the door.

"Hello Uka! What are you up to today? Are you looking for Sissi?" Sissi's mother asked.

"Sissi and I are going on a long bike ride today. We planned it last week. I am so excited! I even packed snacks and drinks for us," Uka said, pointing to his backpack.

"Oh, no," Sissi's mother said. "I think Sissi might have forgotten your plans. She went to Taqu's house to play games this morning."

Uka did not know what to say. He felt like crying. Sissi's mother could see that Uka was upset.

"Uka, do you want me to call Taqu's house so you can talk to Sissi and Taqu? I am sure they would love to have you join them today," said Sissi's mother.

Uka didn't want Sissi's mother to see him upset. Uka just said, "That's okay. I will just go biking by myself."

Uka got back on his bike and pedalled away.

Uka did not feel very good at all. He couldn't believe that Sissi had forgotten their plans together. Uka was also bothered that Taqu and Sissi didn't invite him to play with them.

Uka was hurt. He felt like his friends didn't really care about him.

Uka decided to go biking anyway. He followed the trail past the river.

Uka wanted to try to enjoy the nice day. He had snacks and thought he could have a fun picnic alone.

Uka passed Tuka and Umi at the river. They were both fishing and waved to Uka. They looked like they were having lots of fun. This made Uka feel even worse.

Uka really didn't want to go home, but he wasn't enjoying biking all alone. He was starting to feel like he was going to cry again, and his chest was feeling tight.

Uka realized that he was angry at Sissi for forgetting about him and their plans.

He was also angry at Taqu for making other plans with Sissi and not inviting him along.

Just as Uka was about to turn around and head back home, he saw Miki sitting alone. Miki was in his favourite spot, reading a book. Uka really needed a kind friend to talk with, and Miki was one of the kindest animals Uka knew.

Uka felt better just seeing Miki and decided to bike over to talk with him.

"Hi, Miki," Uka said when he got close enough.

"Hi, Uka. It's nice to see you. It sure is a nice day for a bike ride!" said Miki.

"Uh, I guess it is. Can I sit with you for a bit?"

"Of course you can! Is everything okay?" Miki asked. Miki could tell that something was bothering Uka.

Uka was a little nervous to explain what had happened, because he still felt pretty upset. But he knew it was important to talk with a friend, so he took a deep breath.

"Well, I was supposed to be biking with Sissi. We planned it last week, and I woke up early to make snacks and everything," Uka said, all in one breath.

"That sounds like a fun day you have planned. But where is Sissi?" Miki asked.

"Well, that's the problem! Sissi forgot we had plans, and she made other plans with Taqu. They are playing at Taqu's house, and they didn't even invite me!"

Uka could feel himself getting upset again. "She forgot about me. Sissi is not a good friend!"

Miki could see that Uka's feelings were hurt.

"Maybe Sissi forgot about your plans," Miki suggested. "Sissi and you are really good friends. I'm sure she wouldn't miss your biking day on purpose."

"If Sissi is such a good friend, how could she forget about our plans? How could she forget about me?" Uka said sadly. "If Sissi were a good friend, she would have remembered."

Miki realized that Uka needed to think about it another way.

"Uka, what do you think makes a good friend?" Miki asked.

"I'm not sure. I haven't thought about it," Uka said, considering the question.

"How about you think about the things friends have done that make you feel good or happy?" Miki suggested.

"Well, Aqi can be sad sometimes, but she never forgets about plans she makes or promises. I really like that," said Uka.

"So, you think a friend should be dependable. Is that a good quality?" Miki asked.

"Yes!" Uka answered. "Being dependable is a really good quality in a friend."

Uka thought about friends a bit more. "When I am feeling sad, Umi is really good at making me see things differently. I always feel better when I am around Umi!"

Miki smiled. "So you like when friends make you feel better?"

"Yes. That's really important. We need friends to cheer us up," Uka said.

Uka realized he was feeling a bit better, and he smiled.

Uka thought about his friends a bit more.

"Nauka is really forgiving. Even when I make a mistake, Nauka always gives me another chance. I really like that," Uka said.

"Hmmm, so being forgiving is really important to you?" Miki asked.

"Yes, it is!" Uka said. Then Uka paused for a moment.

"So you think I should be more forgiving to Sissi?" Uka said.

Miki shrugged his shoulders and smiled. "It's up to you, Uka. But I know you and Sissi have been friends for a long time."

33

"I really don't think Sissi would forget your plans on purpose. I think Sissi is going to feel really bad when she realizes she forgot," Miki said.

"You know, I bet Sissi forgot to write down our plans. Her memory is not the best. If she doesn't write things down, she sometimes forgets," said Uka.

Uka paused for a moment, and then added, "I really like spending time with Sissi. I don't want her to feel bad."

Miki nodded. "You are a thoughtful friend. Sissi is lucky to have you as her friend."

Uka was so happy he had talked with Miki. Miki was good at listening and making time for his friends when they needed him.

Uka was feeling a lot better. He realized that he was lucky to have a friend like Miki.

"Thanks, Miki! You are a good friend, too!" Uka said, and he gave his friend a hug. "I am going to bike to Taqu's house and make sure Sissi is not feeling bad about missing our biking day," Uka said. He felt much better than he had all day.

"Do you want to join us, Miki?" Uka asked. "It would be fun to spend more time together."

Miki looked back at his rock and his book. "Thank you for the invitation, Uka! I am really enjoying my book, so I think I will stay here a bit longer."

Uka hugged his friend again before getting on his bike.

Uka pedalled toward Taqu's house as quickly as he could. He didn't want Sissi to feel bad about forgetting their plans for the day.

Nunavummi
Reading Series

The Nunavummi reading series is a Nunavut-developed levelled book series that supports literacy development while teaching readers about the people, traditions, and environment of the Canadian Arctic.

Level 11
- 24–32 pages
- Sentences become complex and varied
- Varied punctuation
- Dialogue is included in fiction texts and is necessary to understand the story
- Readers rely more on the words than the images to decode the text

12
- 24–40 pages
- Sentences are complex and vary in length
- Lots of varied punctuation
- Dialogue is included in fiction texts and is necessary to understand the story
- Readers rely on the words to decode the text; images are present but only somewhat supportive

Level 13
- 24–56 pages
- Sentences can be more complicated and are not always restricted to a structure that readers are familiar with
- Some unfamiliar themes and genres are introduced
- Readers rely on the words to decode the text; images are present but only somewhat supportive

Fountas & Pinnell Text Level: L

This book has been officially levelled using the F&P Text Level Gradient™ Leveling System.